Award

Story by Carmel Reilly
Illustrations by Vasja Koman

A Harcourt Achieve Imprint

www.Rigby.com
1-800-531-5015

It was award day at school.

Josh went along

with his mom and dad

and his big brother Ben.

Dad looked at Josh.

He said,

"Who will get an award today?"

"Ben will get an award," said Josh.

"He always gets one.

He is good at schoolwork."

Josh went and sat down with his friends.

He saw one of the teachers go up on the stage.

The teacher called out the awards.
But Josh did not hear her.
He was deaf.

Josh saw some children
going up to the stage.

He saw Ben get an award.

Josh looked around the room.
He saw his mom and dad.
They smiled at him,
and then they looked at the teacher.

"Josh!" called one of his friends.
"You have an award, too."

"No, not me!" said Josh with a laugh.

"Yes, you," said the boy. "Look! The teacher wants you to go up and get your award."

Josh looked up at the teacher,
and he saw her smiling at him.

Then he looked at his mom and dad
and Ben again.
They all had big smiles.

"Good work," said the teacher.

"Thanks," said Josh, and he smiled, too.